Kiss Your Sister, Rose Marie!

by Nancy White Carlstrom
illustrated by Thor Wickstrom

Macmillan Publishing Company   New York

Maxwell Macmillan Canada   Toronto

Maxwell Macmillan International
New York   Oxford   Singapore   Sydney

Macmillan Publishing Company is part of the
Maxwell Communication Group of Companies
Macmillan Publishing Company
866 Third Avenue
New York, NY 10022

Maxwell Macmillan Canada, Inc.
1200 Eglinton Avenue East
Suite 200
Don Mills, Ontario M3C 3N1

FIRST EDITION
Printed in Hong Kong
10 9 8 7 6 5 4 3 2 1

The text of this book is set in 16 pt. ITC Veljovic Medium.
The illustrations are rendered in pen and ink and watercolor.
Book design by Christy Hale

Library of Congress Cataloging-in-Publication Data
Carlstrom, Nancy White.
Kiss your sister, Rose Marie! / by Nancy White Carlstrom ; illustrated by Thor Wickstrom. — 1st ed.
p.   cm.
Summary: Rose Marie is not at all sure she likes having to deal
with her new sister Baby Boo.
ISBN 0-02-717271-6
[1. Babies—Fiction. 2. Sisters—Fiction.] I. Wickstrom, Thor, ill. II. Title.
PZ7.C21684Ki   1992   [E]—dc20   90-48671

*For big brothers
and big sisters
everywhere*
—N.W.C.

For Jane Margaret
—T.W.

Lucky girl! Lucky girl!
Lucky girl to be the baby!

Mama says, "Be quiet!"
Baby Boo is eating.

Mama says, "Be quiet!"
Baby Boo is sleeping.

Mama says, "Be quiet. Quiet. Quiet. Quiet."

But I want to be **loud**

loud

loud!

I want to thump.
I want to shout.

Get out, Baby Boo! Get out!

Mama says, "That's okay sometimes."

Mama shows me pictures of before.

Rose Marie in baby clothes.
Rose Marie with baby toys.

Rose Marie in a baby bib
making gooey baby noise.

I was the only baby in this house.
And I liked it that way!

Mama says, "That was okay then.
But now, kiss your sister, Rose Marie!"

"Can you make her smile?"
I can make her laugh.

"Kiss your sister, Rose Marie!"

"Can you pat her now?"
I can squeeze real tight.

Squish!

Waah!

"Kiss your sister, Rose Marie!"

"Can you sing a song?"

I can whistle, too.

"Kiss your sister, Rose Marie!"

"Do you know what's wrong?"

I can swing her high.

"Kiss your sister, Rose Marie!"

"Can you let her nap?"

I can tiptoe out.

Bam!

Waah!

"Now get on my lap."

"When you were a baby we sang to you.
When you were a baby we rocked you, too.

When you were a baby we loved you.
We still do!"

Kiss your sister, Baby Boo!